It's Time to Sleep, My Love

ILLUSTRATED BY
Nancy Tillman

WRITTEN BY Eric Metaxas

FEIWEL AND FRIENDS

NEW YORK

"It's time to sleep, it's time to sleep,"
the fishes croon in waters deep.

It's time to sleep   It's time to sleep

The songbirds sing in trees above,
"It's time to sleep, my love, my love."

"It's time to sleep, my love."

"So, go to sleep, my sleepy child,"
the tiger whispers in the wild.

The otter utters by the lake,
"It's getting hard to stay awake."

"So, go to sleep, my love."

"Let's go to sleep, my darling love,"
so coos the sleepy turtledove.

So drones the drowsy bumblebee
inside its hive inside its tree,

it's time to sleep

"Let's go to sleep, my love."

"I'm getting very sleepy now,"
so moos the tired milking cow.

So croaks the almost-sleeping frog
amidst the settling of the fog,

I'm getting very sleepy now

"So, go to sleep, my love."

Your dreams will be arriving soon.
They'll float to you
in sleep's balloon.

They'll be here when I snuff the wick,
you'd better close your eyelids quick.
So you can dream, my love, my love.
So you can dream, my love.

And as you dream inside your sleep,
the fishes crooning in the deep, and
all the songbirds up above
will sleep and dream of you, my love,
of you, the one I love.

It's time to sleep

To Mama, who shared her lap and her love of books with me before I could walk,

and to my wonderful husband, Rick, my biggest cheerleader.

—N.T.

To them, the ones we love.

—E.M.

A FEIWEL AND FRIENDS BOOK
An Imprint of Macmillan

IT'S TIME TO SLEEP, MY LOVE. Text copyright © 2008 by Eric Metaxas. Illustrations copyright © 2008 by Nancy Tillman.
All rights reserved. Printed in June 2011 in China by South China Printing Co. Ltd., Dongguan City, Guangdong Province.
For information, address Feiwel and Friends, 175 Fifth Avenue, New York, N.Y. 10010.

Library of Congress Cataloging-in-Publication Data Available

ISBN: 978-1-250-00290-7

The artwork is created digitally using a variety of software painting programs on a Wacom tablet. Layers of illustrative elements are first individually created,
then merged to form a composite. At this point, texture and mixed media (primarily chalk, watercolor, and pencil) are applied to complete each illustration.

Feiwel and Friends logo designed by Filomena Tuosto

First Edition: 2008

10 9 8 7 6 5 4 3 2 1

mackids.com

Nancy Tillman is the author and illustrator of the bestselling picture book *Wherever You Are, My Love Will Find You;* as well as
On the Night You Were Born; its companion journal, *The Wonder of You: A Book for Celebrating Baby's First Year;*
The Spirit of Christmas; The Crown on Your Head; and *Tumford the Terrible.*

Nancy's mission in creating her books is to convey to children everywhere that "You are loved." She lives in Portland, Oregon.
You can visit her on the Web at www.nancytillman.com.

This special edition was printed for Kohl's Department Stores, Inc. (for distribution on behalf of Kohl's Cares, LLC, its wholly owned subsidiary) by Feiwel and Friends, New York, NY.
978-1-250-00290-7 · Kohl's · 1-250-00290-7 · 123386 · 6/11–10/11

You are loved.